W9-CKG-916

Gg Hh Ii Jj Kk Ll Mm

Ben's ABC Day

Text by Terry Berger

Photographs by Alice Kandell

Lothrop, Lee & Shepard Books • New York

Text copyright © 1982 by Terry Berger
Photographs copyright © 1982 by Alice S. Kandell
All rights reserved. No part of this book may be reproduced
or utilized in any form or by any means, electronic or
mechanical, including photocopying, recording or by any
information storage and retrieval system, without permission
in writing from the Publisher. Inquiries should be addressed
to Lothrop, Lee & Shepard Books, a division of William
Morrow & Company, Inc., 105 Madison Avenue, New York,
New York 10016. Printed in the United States of America.
First Edition.   4 5 6 7 8 9 10

Library of Congress Cataloging in Publication Data
Berger, Terry.
Ben's ABC day.
Summary: A small boy is shown performing
activities beginning with all the letters of the
alphabet.   1. English language—Alphabet—
Juvenile literature.   [1. Alphabet]   I. Kandell,
Alice S., ill. II. Title.
PE1155.B4 [E] 81-13754
ISBN 0-688-00881-X AACR2
ISBN 0-688-00882-8 (lib. bdg.)

For Benjamin Kandell Joseph

A awakening

B brushing

C combing

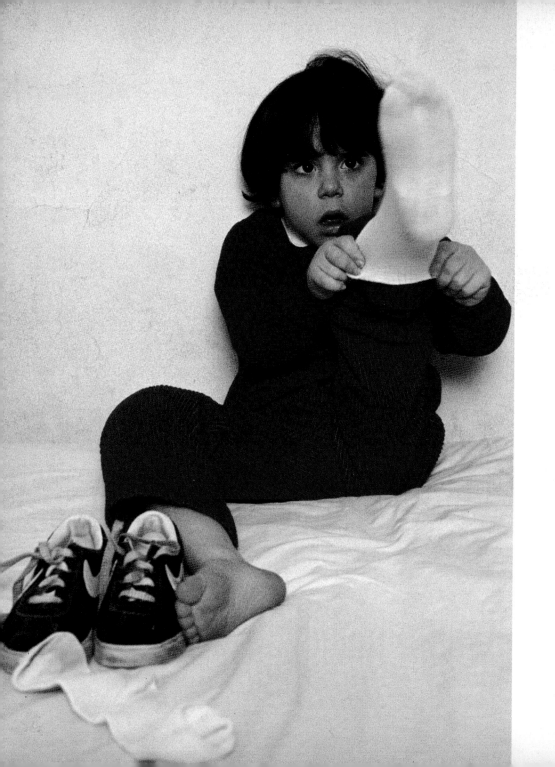

D dressing

E eating

F feeding

G gardening

H helping

I inviting

J joking

K kissing

L licking

M mixing

N nibbling

O opening

P playing

Q questioning

R running

S shopping

T tiring

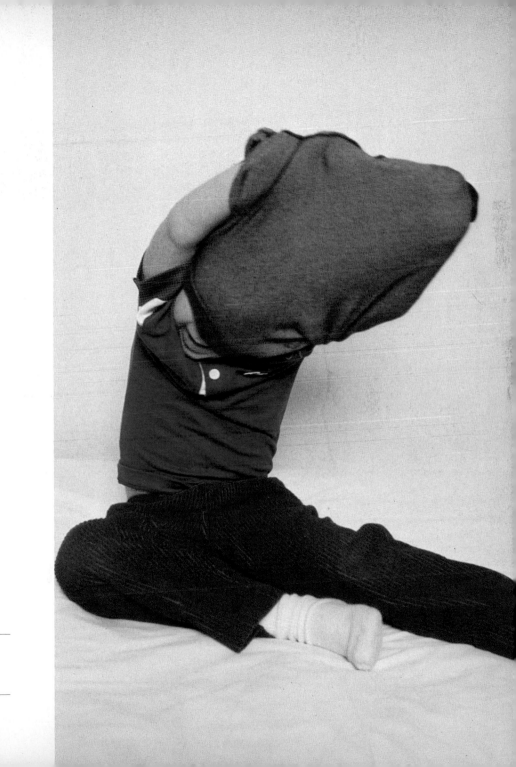

U undressing

V viewing

W washing

X x-ing

Y yawning

Z zzzzzzzzz

TERRY BERGER and ALICE KANDELL worked together to produce a "different alphabet book"—one that would complement others, but would be about "doing things in a child's everyday world." *Ben's ABC Day* is the result of their collaboration.

Terry Berger studied at Vassar College, has taught nursery school, kindergarten, and first grade, has two children of her own, and is the author of many children's books.

Alice Kandell received a doctorate in child psychology at Harvard University and is a professional photographer and writer. The most recent children's books on which she has acted as collaborator/photographer are *Max, the Music-Maker* and *Daddy and Ben Together*, both with Miriam B. Stecher.

Nn Oo Pp Qq Rr Ss T